U0111397

小學漫畫 Grammar 王

Grammar 文法篇 ①

Aman Chiu 著

新雅文化事業有限公司
www.sunya.com.hk

要學好英語，就先掌握
英語文法（grammar）知識！

本書主題

掌握文法（grammar）是學好英語的重要關鍵，本書以文法為主題，共有50個單元，以詞性（word class）角度，率先教授6個文法概念，打好英文基礎！

1. 動詞	2. 情態動詞	3. 形容詞
4. 副詞	5. 介詞	6. 連接詞

漫畫看一看

漫畫以動物島上的一羣學生為主角，透過日常生活趣事帶出文法知識。各課漫畫均會示範正確的英語，形式生動活潑。

Grammar規則你要知

全面解說英文文法知識，內容分為3個欄目：

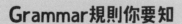

❶ 文法解讀與辨析　❷ 實用例句齊來學　❸ 增潤知識大放送

單元練習及綜合練習

單靠牢記文法知識並不足夠，懂得應用才最重要。本書每個文法概念均設1個單元練習，而書末更附4個綜合練習，鼓勵讀者活學活用，自我檢測學習成果。

綜合練習 2
Integrated exercise 2

Fill in the blanks with the correct modal verb.
請在橫線上填寫正確的情態動詞。

1. Mum says we _____ watch TV after we've finished our homework.
2. His bike broke down in the middle of nowhere, but luckily he _____ to fix it.
3. You _____ leave your door unlocked when you go out.
4. You don't _____ pick me up at the airport. We can get a taxi.
5. I'm not sure what I will do for my holidays, but I _____ go to the beach.
6. Today is your birthday. _____ we go out for dinner tonight?
7. You _____ be tired because you have worked very hard.
8. He _____ love singing, but he doesn't do it any more.
9. How _____ she shout to her mother?
10. _____ you like some coffee or tea?

參考答案：1. can 2. was able 3. shouldn't / oughtn't to 4. need to 5. might / might 6. Shall 7. must 8. used to 9. dare 10. Would

126

綜合練習 3
Integrated exercise 3

There is a mistake in each of the following sentences. Underline and correct them in the spaces provided.
下列句子均有一處錯誤，請在錯誤部分下方畫線，並在橫線上寫出正確答案。

1. I enjoy to talk to my grandparents.
2. It were very kind of him to offer me his coat.
3. Smoke is harmful to your health. You must stop it.
4. My father sometimes lets me going to his office.
5. Please don't make me to stay at this horrible place.
6. Would you mind speak more slowly, please?
7. Are you frighten of spiders?
8. It will be a very excited experience for you.
9. There are lots of butterfly among the flowers.
10. Bill is still ill but he looks a lot more good than the day before.

參考答案：1. to talk → talking 2. were → was 3. Smoke → Smoking 4. going → go 5. to stay → stay 6. speak → speaking 7. frighten → frightened 8. excited → exciting 9. butterfly → butterflies 10. more good → better

127

實用附錄

英語動詞中有很多不規則動詞，其構成方式變化多端。為方便學童學習，本書附不規則動詞表，精選小學階段常用的150個不規則動詞。

Present simple 現在式	Present participle 現在分詞	Past simple 過去式	Past participle 過去分詞
ache (aches) 疼痛	aching	ached	ached
advise (advises) 勸告	advising	advised	advised
agree (agrees) 同意	agreeing	agreed	agreed
apologise (apologises) 道歉	apologise	apologised	apologised
argue (argues) 爭論	arguing	argued	argued
arrange (arranges) 排列	arranging	arranged	arranged
arrive (arrives) 到達	arriving	arrived	arrived
bake (bakes) 焗	baking	baked	baked
be (am / is / are) 是	being	was; were	been
beat (beats) 打敗	beating	beat	beaten / beat
become (becomes) 變成	becoming	became	become
begin (begins) 開始	beginning	began	begun
behave (behaves) 表現	behaving	behaved	behaved
believe (believes) 相信	believing	believed	believed
bend (bends) 弄彎	bending	bent	bent
bite (bites) 咬	biting	bit	bitten
blame (blames) 責備	blaming	blamed	blamed
bleed (bleeds) 流血	bleeding	bled	bled
blow (blows) 吹	blowing	blew	blown
break (breaks) 打碎	breaking	broke	broken
breathe (breathes) 呼吸	breathing	breathed	breathed
bring (brings) 帶來	bringing	brought	brought
build (builds) 建築	building	built	built
burn (burns) 燃燒	burning	burned / burnt	burned / burnt
buy (buys) 購買	buying	bought	bought

130

Present simple 現在式	Present participle 現在分詞	Past simple 過去式	Past participle 過去分詞
catch (catches) 捕捉	catching	caught	caught
chat (chats) 閒談	chatting	chatted	chatted
choose (chooses) 選擇	choosing	chose	chosen
clap (claps) 拍手	clapping	clapped	clapped
close (closes) 關閉	closing	closed	closed
come (comes) 來	coming	came	come
cry (cries) 哭	crying	cried	cried
cut (cuts) 切	cutting	cut	cut
cycle (cycles) 騎車	cycling	cycled	cycled
damage (damages) 破壞	damaging	damaged	damaged
decide (decides) 決定	deciding	decided	decided
decorate (decorates) 裝飾	decorating	decorated	decorated
dig (digs) 挖	digging	dug	dug
do (does) 做	doing	did	done
donate (donates) 捐贈	donating	donated	donated
draw (draws) 繪畫	drawing	drew	drawn
dream (dreams) 做夢	dreaming	dreamed / dreamt	dreamed / dreamt
drink (drinks) 喝	drinking	drank	drunk
drive (drives) 駕駛	driving	drove	driven
eat (eats) 吃	eating	ate	eaten
exercise (exercises) 做運動	exercising	exercised	exercised
fall (falls) 落下	falling	fell	fallen
feed (feeds) 餵飼	feeding	fed	fed
feel (feels) 感覺	feeling	felt	felt
fight (fights) 打架	fighting	fought	fought

131

掌握英語的一個重要方面是理解文法（grammar）。從本質上講，文法是任何語言的基石──它是一套規範我們如何使用單詞組成有意義句子的規則和原則。通過遵守這些規則，我們可以確保溝通清晰，避免誤解。

尤其是在小學階段，掌握英語文法更是通往流利英語的必經之路。但社會上流傳一種觀點，就是認為學英語不用學文法，只要敢開口說就可以了。這固然是一種方法，但它需要為孩子從學齡前開始不斷製造豐富而多樣的學習條件與環境，讓孩子從小便沉浸在濃厚的英語氛圍中，自然而然地學懂英語。

話雖如此，不學文法的結果往往是一口錯漏百出的「流利」英語，有些英語使用者連自己說的話錯在哪裏也不知道，因為他們對文法知識一無所知，自己亦不能分析對錯，但他們可能有一個特別的強項，就是語感。語感是比較直接、迅速地感悟語言文字的能力，它可使人們自然地說出讓人明白的話，寫出讓人明白的句子，在溝通上通行無阻。

那麼我們還要學文法嗎？這答案是肯定的。但是，學文法不能鑽牛角尖，只是牢牢記住文法規則而不去實踐，那是於事無補的。文法是死的，語言是活的；學文法，必須活學活用。歸根究底，文法來自生活，是從語言歸納出來的，所以我們學文法，就必須回到生活，除

了掌握語言的規律，還要學曉語言的語感。我們學文法，不是為了考試，而是為了有一天說話的時候，能忘掉文法規則，脫口而出一口流利正確的英文，這是本書創作的首要原則。本書特色詳述如下：

　　本書按照香港小學課程指引編寫，分兩冊出版，共有 100 課，內容系統全面，詳細歸納小學常用的文法規則。

　　本書從詞性角度，逐一講解動詞、情態動詞、形容詞、副詞、介詞、連接詞的文法知識。

　　每課內容分為 4 個欄目：漫畫看一看、文法解讀與辨析、實用例句齊來學、增潤知識大放送。課前的有趣漫畫吸引學生閱讀，課中詳細講授文法知識，課後還增設練習和附錄以鞏固所學。

　　本書使用簡單易懂的語言，配以中英文例句，力圖使學生以深入淺出的方式掌握小學階段的基礎文法知識，逐步建立正確的英語文法觀念，提高整體英語能力，順利銜接中學課程。

Aman Chiu

人物介紹

歡迎來到動物島！這裏聚居了來自五湖四海的動物，每天都發生大大小小的生活趣事。島上的動物都有一個共通點，就是正在努力學好英文。小朋友，你準備好和一眾動物朋友會面，跟他們一起學英語嗎？

花貓 Emma
天資聰穎，勤奮好學，是學校的模範生。

牛牛 Patrick
愛動腦筋，喜歡閱讀，充滿好奇心。

小鴨 Chris
心地善良，樂於助人，因此人緣很好，很受朋友歡迎。

兔兔 Linda
樂天豁達，平易近人，是朋友眼中的「開心果」。

目錄 Contents

Grammar concept 1 : Verbs 動詞

1 be 動詞
The verb be
14

2 一般動詞
Common verbs
16

3 動詞形式
Verb forms
18

4 不規則動詞
Irregular verbs
20

5 及物與不及物動詞
Transitive and intransitive verbs
22

6 主動詞一致
Subject-verb agreement
24

7 帶 to 的不定詞
To-infinitives
26

8 不帶 to 的不定詞
Bare infinitives
28

9 -ing 形式
The -ing form
30

10 動名詞
Gerunds
32

單元練習 1
Exercise 1
34

Grammar concept 2 : Modals 情態動詞

11 用 can 表示能力
Use *can* to show ability
36

12 用 can 表示請求或許可
Use *can* for requests or permission
38

13 用 could 表示過去的能力
Use *could* to talk about past ability
40

14 用 could 表示請求或請示
Use *could* for requests or permission
42

15 用 may 表示請示或許可
Use *may* to ask for or give permission ... 44

16 用 may / might 表示可能
Use *may* / *might* to show possibility ... 46

17 用 will / would 表示請求、建議或邀請
Use *will* / *would* for requests, offers or invitations ... 48

18 用 must 表示必須
Use *must* to express obligations ... 50

19 用 should / ought to 提出建議
Use *should* / *ought to* for advice ... 52

20 用 shall 提出建議或詢問意見
Use *shall* for suggestions and advice ... 54

21 情態動詞 dare
Use *dare* as a modal ... 56

22 用 used to 表示過去的習慣和狀況
Use *used to* for past habits and situations ... 58

單元練習 2
Exercise 2 ... 60

Grammar concept 3：Adjectives 形容詞

23 形容詞的位置
Positions of adjectives ... 62

24 形容詞的種類
Kinds of adjectives ... 64

25 形容詞的次序
Order of adjectives ... 66

26 以 -ed 和 -ing 結尾的形容詞
Adjectives ending in -ed and -ing ... 68

27 形容詞比較級
Adjectives of comparison ... 70

28 形容詞最高級
Superlative adjectives ... 72

29 比較級和最高級的不規則變化
Irregular comparatives and superlatives ... 74

30 用（not）as…as 作同級比較
Comparison with (not) as…as　　76

31 用作名詞的形容詞
Adjectives as nouns　　78

單元練習 3
Exercise 3　　80

Grammar concept 4：Adverbs 副詞

32 狀態副詞
Adverbs of manner　　82

33 頻率副詞
Adverbs of frequency　　84

34 程度副詞
Adverbs of degree　　86

35 時間副詞
Adverbs of time　　88

36 地方副詞
Adverbs of place　　90

單元練習 4
Exercise 4　　92

Grammar concept 5：Prepositions 介詞

37 時間介詞
Prepositions of time　　94

38 位置介詞
Prepositions of place　　96

39 其他位置介詞
More prepositions of place　　98

40 方向介詞
Prepositions of directions　　100

41 介詞：by
Preposition: by　　102

42 介詞：with
Preposition: with
104

單元練習 5
Exercise 5
106

Grammar concept 6：Conjunctions 連接詞

43 連接詞：and / but / or
Conjunctions: and / but / or
108

44 連接詞：because / so
Conjunctions: because / so
110

45 連接詞：although / though
Conjunctions: although / though
112

46 連接詞：if / unless
Conjunctions: if / unless
114

47 連接詞：before / after
Conjunctions: before / after
116

48 連接詞：when / while
Conjunctions: when / while
118

49 連接詞：until / till
Conjunctions: until / till
120

50 成對使用的連接詞
Conjunctions in pairs
122

單元練習 6
Exercise 6
124

綜合練習1-4　Integrated exercises 1-4
125

實用附錄　Appendix: Irregular verbs
129

Grammar concept 1 : Verbs 動詞

A verb is a word that tells you that someone does something or that something happens or exists.

動詞是用來表示動作、行為或事件發生之詞。

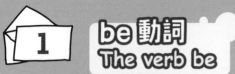

漫畫看一看

❓ 文法解讀與辨析

be 動詞的意思為「是」，它會根據人或事物而有不同變化。

			現在式	過去式
第一人稱	單數	I 我	am	was
	複數	we 我們	are	were
第二人稱	單數	you 你	are	were
	複數	you 你們	are	were
第三人稱	單數	he 他	is	was
		she 她	is	was
		it 它 / 牠	is	was
	複數	they 他們 / 它們 / 牠們	are	were

☑ 實用例句齊來學

- I **am** in the library now. Where **are** you?
  我現在在圖書館裏。你在哪裏呢？

- It **was** a little cold yesterday, but it **is** warm today.
  昨天有點冷，但今天很暖和。

⚠ 增潤知識大放送

英文口語中會用許多縮略形式，如下：

- **I'm** = I am
- **You're** = You are
- **They're** = They are
- **We're** = We are
- **He's / She's / It's** = He is / She is / It is

否定式則加上 not，如下：

- **I ain't / I'm not**
  = I am not

- **You aren't / You're not**
  = You are not

- **We aren't / We're not**
  = We are not

- **They aren't / They're not**
  = They are not

- **He / She / It isn't; He's / She's / It's not** = He / She / It is not

漫畫看一看

❓ 文法解讀與辨析

be 動詞以外的動詞，全都是一般動詞，在句子中用來表示主詞的動作，例如：

dance 跳舞	drink 喝	eat 吃	listen 聽
live 居住	play 玩	read 讀	sit 坐
sleep 睡覺	speak 說	walk 行走	write 寫

✔ 實用例句齊來學

- Let's **eat** pizza today.
  我們今天吃薄餅吧。

- We **play** badminton once a week.
  我們每個星期打一次羽毛球。

- Tom is too shy to ask Lily to **dance** with him.
  湯姆很害羞，不敢邀請莉莉與他共舞。

- **Walk** as fast as you can in order to catch them up!
  有多快走多快，以追上他們！

⚠ 增潤知識大放送

動詞會因不同情況（如時態、人稱等）而出現變化。例如：

- [第一人稱 I] I **scream**. 我尖叫。

- [第二人稱 you] You **scream**. 你尖叫。

- [第三人稱 he, she, it] He **screams**. 他尖叫。

- [現在進行式] She is **screaming**. 她在尖叫。

- [過去式] We **screamed**. 我們當時尖叫了。

漫畫看一看

❓ 文法解讀與辨析

一般動詞有五種形式。動詞按其過去式和過去分詞的構成方式，可分為規則動詞和不規則動詞。規則動詞的過去式和過去分詞一般在詞尾加 ed；結尾是 e 時，只加 d；結尾是 y 時，將 y 改為 ied。

原形動詞	第三人稱單數	現在分詞	簡單過去式	過去分詞
walk	walks	walking	walked	walked
dance	dances	dancing	danced	danced
cry	cries	crying	cried	cried

☑ 實用例句齊來學

- We **learn** English at school. 我們在學校學英語。
- Sandy **learns** Mandarin from her aunt.
  珊迪跟她姨姨學普通話。
- I'm **learning** to play the violin. 我正在學小提琴。
- I **learned** how to swim when I was five. 我五歲時學會了游泳。
- I've **learned** some new English words today.
  我今天學會了幾個英文生字。

⚠ 增潤知識大放送

中文的動詞沒有形式上的變化，例如昨天、今天、明天學習也好，都是用「學習」。英語的動詞卻有許多變化，單看 learn 一詞，在以上例句就有不同面貌。

動詞 learn 的過去式和過去分詞可以是 learned，也可以是 learnt。例如：

- I **learned / learnt** a lot from my parents.
  我從父母那裏學到很多東西。

漫畫看一看

Grammar 規則你要知

❓ 文法解讀與辨析

有些動詞的形式會出現不規則變化。不規則動詞的過去式和過去分詞的變化因詞而異。

原形動詞	第三人稱單數	現在分詞	簡單過去式	過去分詞
buy	buys	buying	bought	bought
speak	speaks	speaking	spoke	spoken
swim	swims	swimming	swam	swum
write	writes	writing	wrote	written

✔ 實用例句齊來學

- I learnt English for years, but I still don't **speak** it very well.
  我學了好多年英語，可是仍然不是說得很好。

- She **speaks** very softly. 她說話聲音非常輕柔。

- Please don't interrupt while someone is **speaking**.
  請別在他人說話時插嘴。

- I **spoke** to them last week. 我上星期跟他們談過了。

- I haven't **spoken** to my parents about all this.
  我還沒有跟父母談過這些事情。

⚠ 增潤知識大放送

動詞 lie 有兩個完全不同的語義，一個會出現規則變化，一個則是不規則變化：

原形動詞	第三人稱單數	現在分詞	簡單過去式	過去分詞
lie 說謊	lies	lying	lied	lied
lie 躺	lies	lying	lay	lain

漫畫看一看

Grammar 規則你要知

❓ 文法解讀與辨析

動詞分為及物動詞（transitive verb）和不及物動詞（intransitive verb）。動詞後面加上動作涉及的人或物是及物動詞，獨立使用的動詞叫不及物動詞。

	主詞	動詞	賓語
及物動詞	Monkey	have	tails.
	He	raised	his hand.
不及物動詞	She	smiled.	X
	The baby	cried.	X

✅ 實用例句齊來學

及物動詞

- Have you **made** your **bed**? 你有沒有把牀鋪好？
- Please **open** the **windows** to let in some fresh air.
  請打開窗戶讓新鮮空氣進來。

不及物動詞

- We are **laughing**. 我們在大笑。
- We need to be quiet because the baby is **sleeping**.
  我們要小聲點，因為寶寶在睡覺。

⚠️ 增潤知識大放送

有些動詞既是及物動詞，又是不及物動詞，例如 sing：

- [及物動詞] We are **singing** a **song**. 我們在唱歌。
- [不及物動詞] We are **singing**. 我們在唱歌。

有時，及物動詞會涉及兩個人或物，例如：

- She **asked** me a **question**. 她問了我一個問題。

因為 question 接受 ask 這個動作，所以是直接受詞（direct object）；而 me 則是間接受詞（indirect object）。

漫畫看一看

Wow! There are many rooms in our school. Some of them are special rooms.

Yes, there is a computer room. There is also an art room. The library is very big.

There're a lot of outdoor facilities, too.

I like the garden on the rooftop the best.

24

❓ 文法解讀與辨析

做動作的人（主詞）和動作（動詞）必須一致，必須兩個同時用單數，或同時用複數。簡單來說，句子裏面的主詞是單數時，後面接的動詞必須是單數動詞；主詞是複數時，後面就要接複數動詞。

✔ 實用例句齊來學

單數

- **She likes** the playground on the roof.
  她喜歡天台的遊樂場。

- **He does** not have a cellphone. 他沒有手機。

- There **is a** tree in the garden. 花園裏有一棵樹。

複數

- **We like** the playground on the roof.
  我們喜歡天台的遊樂場。

- **They do** not have a cellphone. 他們都沒有手機。

- There **are** lots of trees in the garden. 花園裏有很多樹。

⚠ 增潤知識大放送

句子中有兩個主詞時，使用複數動詞。例如：

- **John** and **Mary are** good friends. 約翰和瑪莉是好朋友。

做動作的人（主語）跟動作（動詞）不一定是連着的，我們有時要仔細思考哪兩個部分有關係。在以下句子，pencils 是複數，因此用了表示複數的動詞 are。

- The **pencils** on the table **are** mine. 桌子上的鉛筆是我的。

7 帶 to 的不定詞
To-infinitives

漫畫看一看

26

Grammar 規則你要知

❓ 文法解讀與辨析

在英語中，兩個動詞不能隨意連接在一起。有時我們會在兩個動詞之間加上 to，這叫帶 to 的不定詞（to-infinitive）。

動詞 A		動詞 B
agree		
decide	to	原形動詞
try		
want		

我們很多時用帶 to 的不定詞來表示目的或意願，或是動作和未來的方向。

✔ 實用例句齊來學

- We **agree to go** camping on Sunday. 我們同意周日去露營。
- In the end, we **decided to go** to the cinema. 最後我們決定去看電影。
- She was **trying** not **to cry**. 她強忍住不哭出來。
- What do you **want to eat**? 你想吃什麼？
- I **need to go** to the washroom. 我要去一去洗手間。
- She **hopes to study** abroad. 她希望出國留學。

⚠ 增潤知識大放送

我們說「我想去遊樂場」，其中「想」和「去」兩個動詞連在一起。但在英文裏，我們不能說 I want go to the playground. 動詞 want 和 go 必須用 to 連接起來，即 I want to go to the playground.

不帶 to 的不定詞
Bare infinitives

漫畫看一看

What happened?

I heard something drop and break really loud. I looked into the window but there's nothing.

Then, I heard a woman call for help and a girl cry. That makes me feel so scared.

Calm down, sweetheart. A radio drama is being broadcast.

Silly me!

❓ 文法解讀與辨析

兩個動詞連在一起時，一定要留意第一個動詞是什麼，因為我們以它來決定後面是跟帶 to 或不帶 to 的不定式，還是使用 -ing 形式。

我們會在 make、let 或一些感官動詞（如 see、hear、feel）後面使用不帶 to 的不定詞，即什麼都不用轉變的原形動詞。

動詞 A		動詞 B
make	someone / something 某人或物	原形動詞
let		
see		
hear		
feel		

✓ 實用例句齊來學

- Bob made Anna cry yesterday. 昨天波比把安娜弄哭了。

- Let me go! 讓我走！

- I saw something fall from the sky. 我看到有東西從天上掉下來。

- Did you hear someone knock on the door?
  你有聽到有人在敲門嗎？

- Oh, no! I feel something move around my face!
  噢，不！我感到有東西在臉上移動！

⚠ 增潤知識大放送

感官動詞 smell 後面一般接 -ing 形式，例如：

- Can you smell something burning?
  你聞到有一些東西燒焦的味道嗎？

連接不帶 to 的不定詞還有 watch、notice、observe 等。例如：

- I watched him get into a taxi. 我看着他坐上的士。

漫畫看一看

30

Grammar 規則你要知

❓ 文法解讀與辨析

當兩個動詞連在一起，我們有時會把緊接着的第二個動詞改用 -ing 形式。動詞的 -ing 形式是「名詞化」的動詞，強調動作的連續性。

動詞 A	動詞 B
enjoy	動詞 -ing
finish	
mind	
suggest	

✅ 實用例句齊來學

- He **enjoys** reading long novels. 他喜歡看長篇小說。
- I've **finished** doing my homework. 我已經做完功課了。
- Would you **mind** waiting outside? 請你在外面等好嗎？
- She **suggested** dining out tonight. 她建議今晚外出吃晚飯。

⚠️ 增潤知識大放送

有些動詞後可加不定詞或 -ing 形式，意思都是一樣，例如：

- She **likes** to dance. / She **likes** dancing. 她喜歡跳舞。

但也有意思不同的情況，例如 remember doing something 指「記得曾經做過某事」；而 remember to do something 則指「不要忘記做某事」。比較以下例子：

- I **remember** locking the door. 我記得鎖了門。
- **Remember** to lock the door please. 請記得鎖門。

漫畫看一看

❓ 文法解讀與辨析

我們有時會在動詞後面加 -ing，令它變成名詞。這類詞語叫動名詞（gerund），它擁有跟名詞一樣的功能，常用來表示活動或動作。

動詞	+ -ing =	動名詞
swim		swimming
sing	+ -ing =	singing
play		playing

以上單詞並不能看作是動詞的現在進行式，它們屬於名詞，分別形容游泳、唱歌、玩耍這類活動。

✔ 實用例句齊來學

- Frank is good at **swimming**. 弗蘭克擅長游泳。

- **Listening** to music helps me relax. 聽音樂讓我心情放鬆下來。

⚠ 增潤知識大放送

因為中文並無嚴格區分動詞和名詞，讀者可能會覺得兩者在中文沒有太大的分別，然而在英文是有差別的。

動名詞可作句子的主語（subject）或受詞（object）。

- [主語] **Smoking** is bad for health.
    吸煙危害健康。

- [受詞] My hobbies are **singing** and **dancing**.
    我的嗜好是唱歌和跳舞。

動名詞也可作介詞（preposition）的受詞（object）。

- We look forward to **seeing** you. 我們很期待見到你。

- Alice is good at **playing** the piano. 愛麗絲擅長彈鋼琴。

Fill in the blanks with the correct form of verbs given in the brackets.

請運用括號內的動詞在橫線上填寫正確的動詞形式。

1 When I went home yesterday, it was _____ (get) dark.

2 They _____ (play) basketball every Sunday.

3 I hope _____ (finish) my writing by the end of the day.

4 The bell has _____ (ring), it is time to leave.

5 How _____ (be) you doing?

6 I don't want _____ (talk) about it any more.

7 It was cloudy in the morning, but the sun _____ (be) shining now.

8 Lily _____ (want) to travel because she enjoys _____ (see) new places.

9 Would you mind _____ (help) me?

10 I am planning _____ (have) a party.

Grammar concept 2 :
Modals
情態動詞

A modal verb is a word that is used with another verb to express ideas such as possibility, permission or intention.

情態動詞用在動詞前，表示可能、允許、意願等。

用 can 表示能力
Use *can* to show ability

Grammar 規則你要知

❓ 文法解讀與辨析

我們用 can 來說明技能或能力。表示否定的意思時，會用 cannot 或縮寫 can't。不管是肯定或否定形式，所有情態動詞後面都連接原形動詞。

情態動詞	意思	用法
can	能夠	說明擁有某技能或能力
cannot / can't	不能	說明沒有某技能或能力

✅ 實用例句齊來學

肯定句

- I **can** speak two languages.
  我會說兩種語言。

- Some animals **can** see in the dark.
  有些動物在黑暗中能看見東西。

否定句

- They **cannot** spell the word correctly.
  他們不能把單詞正確地拼寫出來。

- It feels terrible when someone is ill and you **can't** help them. 看到有人生病而你無法幫助他們時，那感覺很糟糕。

⚠️ 增潤知識大放送

can 很多時可以用 be able to 來替代，例如 I can row a boat.（我會划船。）又能說成 I am able to row a boat. 但後者語氣較為正式。

cannot 的縮寫形式 can't，一般用於口語，不適合用在正式寫作上。

用 can 表示請求或許可
Use *can* for requests or permission

漫畫看一看

Grammar 規則你要知

❓ 文法解讀與辨析

我們會用 Can you...? 來請求別人幫忙，用 Can I...? 來請示別人允許，或用 You can / cannot 來表示允許或不允許別人做某事。

句型	意思	用法
Can you...?	你可以……嗎？	請求別人幫忙
Can I...?	我可以……嗎？	請示別人允許
You can / cannot...	你可以 / 不可以……	允許或不允許別人做某事

☑ 實用例句齊來學

請求

- **Can you** help me lift this bag into the boot of the car?
  你能幫我把這個袋放進車尾箱嗎？

請示

- **Can I** borrow your pen? 我可以借用你的筆嗎？

允許 / 不允許

- **You can** use my computer. 你可以使用我的電腦。

- **You cannot** shout in the classroom. 你不可以在課室裏大叫。

⚠ 增潤知識大放送

Can you do me a favour? 用作請求對方幫忙，一般可回答 Sure!（當然！）/ Absolutely!（當然可以！）/ No problem!（沒問題！）/ I'd be happy to!（樂意之至！）/ Yeah, definitely!（好，一定！）

如幫不上忙，就說句 I'm sorry.（不好意思。）

漫畫看一看

Whose championship medals are these?

They're my dad's. When he was young, he could run very fast. He could also swim across the harbour.

What an achievement! Does your dad do any workout now?

Yes, he goes jogging every day.

Hi there!

❓ 文法解讀與辨析

説明過去擁有的能力或會做的事情時，可用 could 來表達。表示否定的意思時，會用 could not 或縮寫 couldn't。不管是肯定或否定形式，所有情態動詞後面都連接原形動詞。could 和 couldn't 亦可分別作為 can 和 can't 的過去式。

情態動詞	意思	用法
could	過去能夠	表示過去的能力
could not / couldn't	過去不能	表示過去沒有的能力
could / couldn't	能 / 不能	作為 can / can't 的過去式

✅ 實用例句齊來學

過去能夠

• Grandma **could** sing very well when she was young.
祖母年輕時唱歌很動聽。

過去不能

• He **couldn't** even speak until he was six.
他直到六歲才會說話。

能 / 不能（過去式）

• You said we **could** play computer games when we finished our homework. 你說過我們完成功課後可以玩電腦遊戲。

⚠️ 增潤知識大放送

could 可以用 was / were able to 來替代，否定式則加上 not。

• She **was able to** run very fast. 她以前跑得很快。

• She **was not able to** speak English. 她以前不會說英語。

用 could 表示請求或請示
Use *could* for requests or permission

❓ 文法解讀與辨析

與 can 一樣，could 也可用來請求別人幫忙，或請示別人允許。但相對於 can，could 表現的語氣更有禮貌，會在較正式的場合使用。

句型	意思	用法
Could you...?	可以請你……嗎？	有禮貌地請求別人幫忙
Could I...?	我可以……嗎？	有禮貌地請示別人允許

✔ 實用例句齊來學

請求幫忙

• **Could you** open the window, please? 可以請你打開窗戶嗎？

• **Could you** pass me the dictionary?
可以請你把字典遞過來嗎？

• **Could you** say thanks to your parents for me?
可以請你代我向你父母道謝嗎？

請示允許

• **Could I** speak to you for a moment? 我可以跟你聊一會嗎？

• **Could I** have more dessert? 我可以多要一點甜品嗎？

• **Could I** have a drink of water, please? 我可以喝點水嗎？

⚠ 增潤知識大放送

向別人求助時，我們可以說 Excuse me, I wonder if you could help me.（不好意思，你可以幫幫我嗎？）通常會先說 Excuse me，那是因為會打擾到對方，說了才提出請求比較有禮貌。

用 may 表示請示或許可
Use *may* to ask for or give permission

Grammar 規則你要知

❓ 文法解讀與辨析

我們用 May I...? 或 May we...? 來禮貌地請求別人同意，
而 may 也可表示允許別人做某事。

句型	意思	用法
May I...? May we...?	我可以……嗎？ 我們可以……嗎？	用於禮貌地請求 別人同意
You may... Someone may...	你可以…… （某人）可以……	表示允許 別人做某事
You may not... Someone may not...	你不可以…… （某人）不可以……	表示不允許 別人做某事

✅ 實用例句齊來學

請求同意

- **May I** have a glass of warm water? 我可以要一杯暖水嗎？
- **May we** go home now, please? 請問我們現在可以回家嗎？

允許／不允許

- **You may** take a rest now. 你現在可以休息一下。
- **Students may not** use cellphones in school.
  學生不可在學校裏用手機。

⚠️ 增潤知識大放送

May I / we...? 是一種客氣的請求，例如在餐廳點餐時，
我們可以對侍應說 May I / we have the menu, please?
（可以給我們餐牌嗎？）對方一般會回覆：Sure! Here
you go.（當然！餐牌在這裏。）

又例如，結賬時我們可以說 May I / we have the bill,
please?（可以給我賬單嗎？）

漫畫看一看

46

Grammar 規則你要知

❓ 文法解讀與辨析

我們會用 may 和 might 來表示有可能發生的事情，兩者意思大致相同，但有些人認為 might 的語氣比 may 要猶豫一些。表示否定的意思時，會用 may not 或 might not。

情態動詞	意思	用法
may / might	可能；大概；也許	表示有可能發生的事情
may not / might not	不可能；大概不	表示不太可能發生的事情

✅ 實用例句齊來學

肯定句

• I **may / might** go to the cinema later on.
我一會兒可能會去看電影。

否定句

• Mum **may not / might not** join us for dinner tonight.
今晚媽媽可能不會和我們一起吃晚餐。

⚠️ 增潤知識大放送

may 和 might 用於推測，說話者並不確定所說的話是否真確，有時候我們可以用 perhaps（也許）來替代，例如 She may know the answer.（她可能會知道答案。）可以說成 Perhaps she knows the answer.

may 和 might 後接 be + 動詞進行式時，表示動作正在進行或將要發生，例如：

• They **may / might be going** abroad next month.
他們可能下個月出國。

漫畫看一看

Grammar 規則你要知

❓ 文法解讀與辨析

我們會用 will 和 would 來表示請求、建議或邀請。兩者的差異在於 would 較為禮貌、委婉、客氣和正式。

句型	意思	用法
Will you...? Would you...?	請……好嗎？	用於請求別人做某事。
Will you...? Would you...?	要不要……？	用於向某人提出建議或邀請某人。

✔ 實用例句齊來學

請求

- Turn on the air-con, **will you**? 請開冷氣好嗎？

- **Would you** pass me the book? 請把書本傳過來好嗎？

- **Would you** please tell me the way to the library?
  請告訴我如何去圖書館好嗎？

提出建議或邀請

- **Will you** have some more tea? 你要不要再喝多些茶？

- **Would you** like some snacks? 你要不要吃些小食？

- We're going to have a party tonight. **Would you** be interested in coming?
  我們今晚會開派對，你有沒有興趣一起來？

⚠ 增潤知識大放送

有時我們會用否定疑問句 Won't you...? 來提出邀請或請求。例如：

- **Won't you** take off your coat? 你要不要把大衣脫掉？

- **Won't you** come in and have something to drink?
  你要不要進來喝點什麼？

漫畫看一看

We must hurry, or we'll miss the ferry and the football match!

It's late! We mustn't miss the ferry, or we'll have to wait for the next one.

I left my wallet in the library and I have to go back.

Just give me ten minutes. I'll be right back.

Grammar 規則你要知

❓ 文法解讀與辨析

我們會用 must 來說必須做的事情，表示否定的意思時用 must not 或縮寫 mustn't。

情態動詞	意思	用法
must	必須	表示必須做某事
must not / mustn't	絕不能	表示絕不能做某事

✔ 實用例句齊來學

肯定句

- It's very late. I **must** go now. 很晚了，我現在得走了。

- Everyone **must** keep quiet during the exam.
  考試期間必須保持安靜。

否定句

- We **must not** play on the road. 我們絕不能在馬路上玩耍。

- Students **mustn't** be late for school. 學生上學絕不能遲到。

⚠ 增潤知識大放送

must 通常可用 have to 來取代，例如 You must behave yourself.（你要乖一點。）可以說成 You have to behave yourself.

must 還有另外一個意思，指「肯定；一定」，用來表示推測。這個時候，否定式不是 mustn't，而是 can't，例如：

- [肯定式] Lily told me she had arrived. That girl on the bench **must** be Lily.
  莉莉告訴我她到了，那個坐在長凳上的女孩一定是莉莉。

- [否定式] Lily is out of town. That girl on the bench **can't** be Lily.
  莉莉不在城裏，那個坐在長凳上的女孩不可能是莉莉。

用 should / ought to 提出建議
Use *should / ought to* for advice

❓ 文法解讀與辨析

我們會用 should 或 ought to 來建議應該做的事情，表示否定的意思時用 should not（縮寫是 shouldn't）或 ought not to。

情態動詞	意思	用法
should / ought to	應該；應當	表示應該做某事
should not / shouldn't / ought not to	不應	表示不應該做某事

✔ 實用例句齊來學

肯定句

- We **should** respect our parents. 我們應該尊敬父母。
- If you are sick, you **ought to** see a doctor.
  如果你生病了，就應該去看醫生。

否定句

- We **should not** shout in the library. 我們不應在圖書館大叫。
- Students **ought not to** behave rudely. 學生不應作出粗魯的行為。

⚠ 增潤知識大放送

should 和 ought to 可互相替換，但一般來說，前者比較常用，後者則比較正式。例如：

- [一般場合] "You **should** do more exercise to keep fit," said Tom to his friend. 湯姆對朋友說：「你應該多做運動來減重。」
- [正式場合] "For the sake of health, you **ought to** do more exercise," said the doctor to his patient.
  醫生對病人說：「為了健康着想，你應當多做運動。」

在疑問句中，should 用來徵求別人的建議，例如：

- What **should** I do when I see a car accident?
  看到交通意外時，我應該怎麼辦？

Grammar 規則你要知

❓ 文法解讀與辨析

我們用 Shall we / I…? 來有禮貌地提出建議，還會用 What shall we / I…? 來詢問別人的意見。

句型	意思	用法
Shall we / I…?	我們 / 我……好嗎？	提出建議
What shall we / I…?	我們 / 我該……呢？	詢問意見

✔ 實用例句齊來學

提出建議

- Shall I turn on the lights? 我開燈好嗎？

- Shall we meet again next weekend?
  我們下周末要不要再見面？

詢問意見

- What shall I get for dinner? 晚飯我該做什麼來吃？

- We're running out of time. What shall we do?
  時間不多了，我們該怎麼辦？

⚠ 增潤知識大放送

Shall we go to the movies?（我們去看電影好嗎？）是美式英語的說法，英式英語的說法是 Shall we go to the cinema?

表示徵求對方意見或請求時，shall 也可用於第三人稱作主語的疑問句中。例如：

- Shall my son carry the bag for you?
  讓我兒子幫你提那個袋好嗎？

- Shall Yoyo attend the conference tomorrow?
  讓瑤瑤明天出席會議好嗎？

情態動詞 dare
Use *dare* as a modal

Grammar 規則你要知

❓ 文法解讀與辨析

dare 表示敢於做危險或害怕的事情，一般用於否定句或某些特別句型。

句型	意思	用法
dare not / daren't + 原形動詞	不敢	表示不敢做某事
How dare...? / Dare...!	竟敢、膽敢	表示語氣憤怒或震驚

✔️ 實用例句齊來學

否定句

- I **dare not** tell Mum that I've broken the vase.
  我不敢告訴媽媽我把花瓶摔破了。

- She **daren't** tell her secrets to anyone.
  她不敢把自己的秘密告訴任何人。

特別情況

- **How dare** you talk to your parents like that?
  你膽敢這樣跟你父母說話？

- **Dare** you take my wallet without my permission!
  你竟敢沒有問我就拿走我的錢包！

⚠️ 增潤知識大放送

dare 本來是動詞，但用作情態動詞時，就不會有任何時態或形式變化，後面可直接加上原形動詞。例如我們會說 She dare not tell the truth. （她不敢說出真相。）而不說 She dares not tell the truth.

I dare say 用於口語中，意思是「我認為；我想」，例如：

- You're tired, **I dare say**. 我看你是累了。

漫畫看一看

Do you swim a lot?

Not now, but I used to swim a lot a few years ago.

Do you see the villas over there?

There used to be a beach over there. I've seen dolphins jumping out of the water.

Yes, they look luxurious.

I wish I could see them too!

❓ 文法解讀與辨析

我們用 used to 來說過去經常做的事或過去的狀況，而這些事情或狀況現在已不存在了。

情態動詞	意思	用法
used to	過去慣常 / 經常……	表示過去經常做的事
	以前是……的	表示過去的狀況

✔ 實用例句齊來學

過去經常做的事

- I **used to** drink coffee a lot.
  我以前經常喝很多咖啡。

- Mr Chan **used to** swim every day when he was young.
  陳先生小時候每天都會游泳。

- They don't come and see us like they **used to**.
  他們不像過去那樣經常來看我們了。

過去的狀況

- She **used to** be a good friend of mine.
  她曾是我的好朋友。

- They **used to** live in an enormous mansion in the mountain.
  他們以前住在山上的大豪宅。

⚠ 增潤知識大放送

used to 是固定說法，不能說成 use to 或 be used to。例如我們會說 I used to swim a lot.（我以前常常游泳。）而不說 I use to / was used to swim a lot. 但在問句形式就可說：Did you use to swim a lot?（你以前經常游泳嗎？）

Choose the correct modal verb for the following sentences. Tick the correct box.

請為下列句子選出正確的情態動詞，並在 ☐ 內加 ✓。

1 (☐ A. Could ☐ B. Will ☐ C. Dare) I speak to Mrs Wong, please?

2 You (☐ A. mustn't ☐ B. daren't ☐ C. wouldn't) leave litter lying around.

3 (☐ A. Could ☐ B. Should ☐ C. Would) you like some cake?

4 Take an umbrella. It (☐ A. could ☐ B. might ☐ C. should) rain later.

5 "(☐ A. Should ☐ B. May ☐ C. Might) I ask a question?" "Yes, of course."

6 Drivers (☐ A. must ☐ B. ought ☐ C. can) stop when the traffic lights are red.

7 (☐ A. Should ☐ B. May ☐ C. Could) you lend me your bike for the weekend?

8 Mum (☐ A. can ☐ B. will ☐ C. dare) get angry if I come home late.

9 How (☐ A. could ☐ B. ought ☐ C. dare) you suggest he was lazy!

10 Janet (☐ A. could ☐ B. used to ☐ C. would) love diving, but she doesn't do it any more.

參考答案：1. A 2. A 3. C 4. B 5. B 6. A 7. C 8. B 9. C 10. B

Grammar concept 3：
Adjectives
形容詞

An adjective is a word that describes someone or something.

形容詞用來描述人或事物的性質。

漫畫看一看

Grammar 規則你要知

❓ 文法解讀與辨析

我們會用形容詞描述一件物件的外觀或給我們的感覺。英文形容詞會放在不同的位置，它有時會在名詞前面，有時會在 be 動詞後面，有時會在與感官有關的動詞後面。

位置	例子	
名詞前面	**a thick book** 厚的書	**a beautiful girl** 漂亮的女孩
be 動詞後面	**He** is angry. 他很憤怒。	**She** is sad. 她很傷心。
感官動詞後面	**I** feel good. 我感覺很好。	**It** tastes awful. 味道差劣。

✔ 實用例句齊來學

名詞前面

- Who is that **tall boy**? 那個子高的男孩是誰？
- Marie Curie was a **famous scientist**. 居禮夫人是著名的科學家。

be 動詞後面

- The dim sum here **is delicious**. 這裏的點心很好吃。
- It **was** very **hot** yesterday. 昨天很熱。

感官動詞後面

- My eyes **feel sore**. 我的眼睛很痛。
- Grandpa **seems tired**. 祖父好像累了。

⚠ 增潤知識大放送

感官動詞（verbs of perception）用來描述人的感官動作。常用的感官動詞有 look（看起來）、sound（聽起來）、smell（聞起來）、taste（嘗起來）、feel（摸起來；感覺起來）、seem（似乎）等。

漫畫看一看

Look! There's a yellow dragon with a very long tail flying in the red sky!

The dragon has a pair of beautiful wings.

Is it a Chinese dragon or a western dragon?

I have no idea. Everything just looks so weird.

Grammar 規則你要知

❓ 文法解讀與辨析

描述事物時，我們可以從大小（size）、顏色（colour）、形狀（shape）、國籍或產地（nationality / origin）、物料（material）、給人的感覺或特徵（opinion / quality）等方面着手，把它準確地描繪出來。

✔ 實用例句齊來學

大小

• They live in a **small** / **big** house. 他們住在一棟小 / 大房子裏。

顏色

• The dress was **dark blue** / **bright red**.
這條連身裙是深藍色 / 鮮紅色的。

形狀

• She has a **round** / **oval** face. 她有一塊圓圓的臉 / 鵝蛋臉。

國籍或產地

• Do you prefer a **Korean** or **Chinese** cellphone?
你喜歡韓國製手機還是中國製手機？

物料

• She bought a **wooden** / **glass** table. 她買了一張木 / 玻璃桌子。

給人的感覺或特徵

• The **beautiful** flowers have a **nice** smell.
這些美麗的花朵氣味芬芳。

⚠ 增潤知識大放送

與物料有關的字詞還包括：plastic（塑膠製的）、metal（金屬製的）、silk（絲綢製的）、paper（紙製的）、cotton（棉製的）等。例如：

• These **plastic** cups are biodegradable. 這些塑膠杯可生物降解。

漫畫看一看

❓ 文法解讀與辨析

為了給事物提供更豐富的資訊，有時候我們會連用兩個或以上的形容詞。表示意見的形容詞一般放在前面，描述事實的形容詞則放在後面。描述事實的形容詞一般按以下次序列出。

形容詞							名詞
意見	事實						
	Size 大小	Age 年歲	Shape 形狀	Colour 顏色	Origin 產地	Material 物料	

✅ 實用例句齊來學

- [意見 + 大小 + 顏色] They live in a **lovely big green** house.
  他們住在一所美麗的綠色大房子裏。

- [大小 + 形狀 + 顏色] Aunt Amy has a **big fat white** dog.
  艾美姨姨養了一隻又大又肥的白狗。

- [年歲 + 顏色 + 物料] She always wears a pair of **old brown leather** trousers.
  她總是穿着一條舊的棕色皮褲子。

⚠ 增潤知識大放送

如果依照以上的形容詞順序排列，我們可以造出以下句子：

- [意見 + 大小 + 年歲 + 形狀 + 顏色 + 產地 + 物料] She bought a pair of **lovely little old oval green Chinese jade** earrings.
  她買了一對可愛、小巧、古老的橢圓形綠色中國翡翠耳環。

但其實我們描述事物時，一般使用二至四個形容詞已經很足夠；再多的話，句子便會變得冗長和難以閱讀。

漫畫看一看

Grammar 規則你要知

❓ 文法解讀與辨析

不少形容詞會成雙成對地出現，它們以 -ed 或 -ing 來結尾，
分別用來指人和事物。例子如下：

指人	指事物	指人	指事物
bored 感到沉悶的	boring 令人沉悶的	interested 感興趣的	interesting 引起興趣的
frightened 感到驚慌的	frightening 令人驚慌的	annoyed 感到厭煩的	annoying 令人厭煩的
worried 感到擔心的	worrying 令人擔心的	amazed 感到驚訝的	amazing 令人驚訝的

☑ 實用例句齊來學

指人

• Everyone was **excited** when the bride came into the church.
新娘步進教堂時，大家都感到很興奮。

指事物

• I enjoyed the roller coaster ride. It was quite exciting.
這個過山車很好玩，真是太刺激了。

⚠ 增潤知識大放送

bored 與 boring 或 interested 與 interesting 的用法很容易
混淆。它們都是形容詞，但 bored 與 interested 用來指人，
例如我覺得很沉悶或感興趣；而 boring 與 interesting 則指事
物，即它很沉悶或有趣。例如：

• Jeff is **interested** in science.
傑夫對科學感興趣。

• Jeff always has a lot of interesting ideas.
傑夫總是有很多有趣的想法。

漫畫看一看

How many brothers and sisters do you have?

I have one elder brother and one younger sister.

I'm an only child. I always fancy having a big family.

My brother is one year older than I and my sister is three years younger than I.

Yet, sometimes it's annoying to look after my baby sister. She cries day and night.

❷ 文法解讀與辨析

比較兩個性質相同的事物時，就會用到形容詞的比較級。
形容詞轉換成比較級時，需遵從以下規則。

形容詞	比較級規則		例句
單音節	詞尾加 **-er**		A is shorter than B. A 比 B 矮。
單音節， 以 **e** 結尾	詞尾加 **-r**		A is larger than B. A 比 B 大。
單音節，以短母音 或單子音結尾	重複最後字母， 詞尾再加 **-er**	**+ than**	A is thinner than B. A 比 B 瘦。
雙音節， 以 **y** 結尾	去 y， 詞尾再加 **-ier**		A is heavier than B. A 比 B 重。
雙音節或 多音節	形容詞前方 加 **more**		A is more beautiful than B. A 比 B 漂亮。

☑ 實用例句齊來學

- My brother is **younger than** me. 弟弟年紀比我小。

- We need a **larger** fridge. 我們需要一部更大的冰箱。

- Their house is **bigger than** ours. 他們的房子比我們的大。

- John seems a lot **happier** since he quit his job.
  約翰自離職後似乎快樂多了。

- His model car is **more expensive than** mine.
  他的模型車比我的貴。

⚠ 增潤知識大放送

比較級前面還可以用 a lot（許多）、much（遠超過）、a little
（有點）等來突顯兩個事物的分別。例如：

- You look **a little** fatter. Have you gained weight?
  你看來長胖了一點，你體重有增加嗎？

漫畫看一看

❓ 文法解讀與辨析

比較三個或以上的性質相同的事物時，我們會用最高級來表示「最⋯⋯的一個」。形容詞轉換成最高級時，需遵從以下規則。

	形容詞	最高級規則	例子
the +	單音節	詞尾加 -est	the shortest 最矮的
	單音節， 以 e 結尾	詞尾加 -st	the largest 最大的
	單音節，以短母音 或單子音結尾	重複最後字母， 詞尾再加 -est	the thinnest 最瘦的
	雙音節， 以 y 結尾	去 y， 詞尾再加 -iest	the heaviest 最重的
	雙音節或 多音節	形容詞前方 加 most	the most beautiful 最漂亮的

✔ 實用例句齊來學

- Bella is **the cleverest** student in the school.
  貝拉是全校最聰明的學生。

- What is **the highest** mountain in the world?
  世界上哪座山最高？

- It's **the most exciting** TV drama I've ever seen.
  這是我看過最刺激的電視劇。

⚠ 增潤知識大放送

最高級形容詞的前面還可以用 by far（⋯⋯得多；最）等，來進一步加強語氣。例如：

- They are **by far** the most intelligent students in town, winning trophies in inter-school quiz competitions.
  他們是城中最聰明絕頂的學生，在校際問答比賽中獲勝。

漫畫看一看

George is the best in Maths in our class.

Yes, he can do the most difficult sums quickly and accurately.

Mine are even worse.

But no one is perfect. He is poor at Art. His drawings are the worst I've ever seen.

You're just being humble. I think you can draw better than him.

❓ 文法解讀與辨析

有些形容詞的比較級和最高級不是在後面加上 -er 或 -est，也不是在前面加上 more 或 most，例如 good 和 bad，請看下表。

形容詞	比較級	最高級
good 好	better 好一些	best 最好
bad 差；壞	worse 差一些；壞一些	worst 最差；最壞

✔ 實用例句齊來學

比較級

- The novel was **better than** I expected.
  這部小說比我預期的好看。

- If the weather gets any **worse**, we'll have to go back.
  如果天氣再轉壞，我們就只好回去了。

最高級

- Some of **the best** dim sums come from this restaurant.
  一些最好吃的點心來自這家餐廳。

- That was **the worst** burger I've ever eaten.
  那是我吃過的最難吃的漢堡包。

⚠ 增潤知識大放送

形容詞最高級 best 前方可用所有格（如 my、his、their），此時不加 the。例如：

- Sam is **my best** friend. 森是我最好的朋友。

- This cocert is one of **our best** performances ever!
  這場演唱會是我們有史以來最好的表演之一！

用（not）as … as 作同級比較
Comparison with (not) as … as

漫畫看一看

❓ 文法解讀與辨析

我們用 A is as + 形容詞 + as B 來說明 A 和 B 在某方面是相同的。如果想表達否定，就用 A is not as + 形容詞 + as B。

句型	比較級	最高級
as … as	A 像 B 一樣……	表示 A 和 B 在某方面是相同的
not as … as	A 不像 B 那樣……	表示 A 在某方面不如 B

☑ 實用例句齊來學

肯定句

- Mia is **as tall as** Emma. 米雅跟愛瑪一樣高。

- The English test is **as easy as** the Maths test.
  英文測驗像數學測驗那樣容易。

否定句

- David is **not as strong as** Charles. 大衛沒有查理斯那麼強壯。

- Her eyes are **not as big as** her mother's.
  她的眼睛沒有像她媽媽那麼大。

⚠ 增潤知識大放送

我們可以加上倍數來突顯程度。例如：

- His house is twice **as big as** hers. 他的房子是她的兩倍大。

- Her car is three times **as expensive as** his.
  她車子的價格是他的三倍。

英語中有不少比喻，是用「as + 形容詞 + as + 動物」來組成的。例如：

- **as brave as a lion** 勇猛如獅

- **as strong as a horse** 健壯如牛

❓ 文法解讀與辨析

某些形容詞前加上定冠詞 the，可變成名詞來表示人。

表示某類人	
the poor 窮人 (= poor people)	the rich 富人 (= rich people)
the old / the elderly 老人 (= old people)	the young 年輕人 (= young people)
the blind 盲人 (= blind people)	the deaf 聾人 (= deaf people)

表示某國籍的人	
the Chinese 中國人 (= Chinese people)	the American 美國人 (= American people)
the British 英國人 (= British people)	the Japanese 日本人 (= Japanese people)
the German 德國人 (= German people)	the Indian 印度人 (= Indian people)

✔ 實用例句齊來學

- To heal **the wounded** is our duty. 拯救傷者是我們的責任。

- The nurse is caring for **the sick**. 那護士正在照顧病人。

- Please donate generously to help **the poor**.
  請慷慨解囊，以幫助窮人。

- **The young** should show respect to **the elderly**.
  年輕人應該尊敬長者。

- I heard **the French** like to drink wine. 聽說法國人喜歡喝酒。

- **The Chinese** make excellent high-speed trains.
  中國人生產的高速列車性能優良。

⚠ 增潤知識大放送

在形容詞前面加上 the，也可表示一類事物或抽象概念。例如：

- **The new** is to take the place of **the old**.
  新事物最終會取代舊事物。

There is a mistake in each of the following sentences.
Circle and correct them in the spaces provided.

下列句子均有一處錯誤，請圈起錯誤的部分，並在橫線
上寫上正確答案。

1 My brother thinks he's intelligenter than me, but I don't agree.

_____

2 This is probably the most bad TV programme I've ever seen.

_____

3 What is the most dry month of the year in Hong Kong?

_____

4 A young pretty girl walked into the room.

_____

5 He bought a British wollen fabulous suit.

_____

6 My uncle adopted a beautiful grey big bulldog.

_____

7 These villas belong to the riched and famous.

_____

8 It may be better for the sicks to be cared for at home rather than in hospital.

_____

參考答案：1. intelligenter → more intelligent 2. most bad → worst
3. most dry → driest 4. young pretty → pretty young
5. British wollen fabulous → fabulous British wollen
6. grey big → big grey 7. riched → rich 8. sicks → sick

Grammar concept 4 :
Adverbs
副詞

An adverb is a word that tells you how, when or where something is done.

副詞用來表示方式、時間、地點等。

漫畫看一看

Grammar 規則你要知

❓ 文法解讀與辨析

狀態副詞告訴我們事情或動作是如何進行的,它通常放在動詞後面。一般來說,只要將形容詞字尾加上 -ly,即可變成狀態副詞,但有些特殊的副詞變化要注意一下。

規則	形容詞	狀態副詞
直接加 -ly	quick	quickly 很快地
直接加 -y	full	fully 完全地
去 y,加 -ily	easy	easily 容易地
去 e,加 -ly	comfortable	comfortably 舒服地
同形不變	early hard fast	early 提早 hard 艱難地 fast 快捷地
不規則變化	good	well 很好地

✔ 實用例句齊來學

- Let's walk **quickly** in order to get there on time.
  我們走快一點,要準時趕到那裏。

- Has Grandpa **fully** recovered from his illness?
  爺爺完全康復了嗎?

- If you finish **early**, you can go home.
  如果你提前完成,你可以回家。

⚠ 增潤知識大放送

不少副詞都是以 -ly 結尾,但有些字的末尾雖然是 -ly,卻不是副詞,而是形容詞,例如 ugly(醜陋的)、friendly(友善的)、lovely(可愛的)、lonely(孤獨的)。

- The lonely man walked **lonelily** along the road.
  那孤獨的男子孤獨地走在路上。

漫畫看一看

❷ 文法解讀與辨析

頻率副詞用以表示事情發生的頻密程度，下表的副詞按次數多少由上至下順序排列。

發生頻率	頻率副詞
100%	always 總是
	usually 通常
	often 常常
	sometimes 有時
	seldom 很少
0%	never 從不

✔ 實用例句齊來學

- You should **always** brush your teeth before breakfast.
  你必須在吃早餐前刷牙。

- We **usually** have lunch at a nearby Chinese restaurant on Sundays. 我們通常在星期天去附近的中式茶樓吃午飯。

- They **sometimes** go to the beach in summer.
  他們在夏天有時會去沙灘。

- He **seldom** does exercise, so he becomes overweight.
  他很少做運動，所以他超重了。

⚠ 增潤知識大放送

頻率副詞通常放在動詞前面，例如：

- I **usually arrive** home at about six o'clock.
  我通常六時左右回到家裏。

但動詞是 be 時，頻率副詞就會放在後面，例如：

- I **am always** happy. 我總是很快樂。

漫畫看一看

I'm quite worried about the mid-term test tomorrow.

You're a very good student. You did extremely well in the last school term. Why are you so nervous?

I got sick last week. I didn't have time to prepare for the test. I'm really nervous.

No worries. You'll be fine.

Grammar 規則你要知

❓ 文法解讀與辨析

我們用程度副詞來使詞語的意思變得更強烈或更微弱，下表的副詞按強弱程度由上至下順序排列。

強弱程度	程度副詞
最強	extremely 極度；incredibly 難以置信地
	very 非常；really 真的
	too 太；quite 相當；so 很
	slightly 稍微；a little 有點
最弱	hardly 幾乎不

✔ 實用例句齊來學

- He plays the piano **extremely** well. 他彈鋼琴彈得極好。
- This veggie pizza is **really** nice. 這個素薄餅真好吃。
- The background music is **too** loud. 背景音樂太大聲了。
- She is **slightly** underweight. 她稍微過輕。
- It is very dark and everything is **hardly** visible.
  太黑了，幾乎看不見任何東西。

⚠ 增潤知識大放送

程度副詞主要會放在 be 動詞或一般動詞後面，或在被修飾的形容詞前面。例如：

- You **look so** nice in this skirt. 妳穿這條半身裙很好看。
- The water was **extremely cold**. 水非常冷。

程度副詞也可以放在副詞前面，用來修飾副詞。例如：

- They speak **too loudly** that I couldn't hear what you say.
  他們說話太大聲了，我聽不到你說什麼。

漫畫看一看

Are you not going to the field trip tomorrow?

No, I just moved into my new house yesterday. I need to unpack this week.

I heard you're going to change school soon, is that so?

Not this year. Maybe next year. I've got to go now. Talk to you later.

❓ 文法解讀與辨析

時間副詞指出事情或動作在什麼時候發生。

時間副詞
just 剛剛
now 現在
soon 快要、馬上
later 晚一點
last 上個　this 這個　next 下個　＋　week 星期　month 月　或其他時間
yesterday / today / tomorrow 昨天 / 今天 / 明天

✅ 實用例句齊來學

- We **just** went ice skating. 我們剛剛去了溜冰。
- I'm very hungry **now**. 我現在很餓。
- I will call you back **later**. 我晚一點回撥電話給你。
- We had a buffet dinner **last night**. 我們昨晚吃了自助餐。
- They'll come visit us **tomorrow**. 他們明天會來探望我們。

⚠️ 增潤知識大放送

時間副詞一般放在句尾，但有時會放在句子開首以作強調。例如：

- **Yesterday**, I went to the cinema. 昨天，我去了看電影。

在 last、this、next、yesterday、today、tomorrow 前面，不用加任何詞語連接句子，例如：

- I'll see you **next Monday**. 下周一見。
- We went to Japan **last winter**. 去年冬天我們去了日本。

❓ 文法解讀與辨析

地方副詞放在動詞後面，説明事情或動作發生的地點。

地方副詞
in 向裏面；out 向外面
away 遠去；back 回來
here 在這裏；there 在那裏
upstairs 樓上；downstairs 樓下
inside 裏面；outside 外面

✅ 實用例句齊來學

- Get **out**! 出去！

- The parrot flew **away**, and then it flew **back**.
  鸚鵡飛走了，然後又飛回來。

- Stay **here**. I'll go **there**. 待在這兒，我到那邊去。

- The students went **upstairs** to their classroom.
  學生走到樓上課室去。

- They went **outside** to the park so they could play.
  他們到外面的公園去了，這樣他們就可以玩耍。

⚠️ 增潤知識大放送

地方副詞不一定只能用來修飾動作，它們也可以放在名詞後面，修飾人或事物。例如：

- The people **here** are very nice. 這裏的人很親切。

here 和 there 是最常用的地方副詞，有時會把它們放在句子開頭，以加強語氣或發出感歎，例如：

- **Here** comes the train! 火車來了！

- **There** you go again! 你又來了！

單元練習 4
Exercise 4

Fill in the blanks with the suitable adverb from the table given below.

請從下表選擇合適的副詞，填在橫線上。

seldom	merrily	extremely	downstairs	here
outside	lazily	well	often	tommorow

1 The dog sat in the shade of the tree _____ .

2 I _____ visit my grandparents at weekends.

3 It's _____ hot today. Please turn on the air conditioner.

4 They are standing _____ the classroom.

5 The children laughed _____ .

6 My mother told me not to go away. I'm waiting for her _____ .

7 I don't have time now. I'll do it _____ .

8 I went to open the door _____ .

9 Now that we can pay to watch most of the films on TV, we _____ go to the cinema.

10 I couldn't sleep very _____ last night.

參考答案：1. lazily   2. often   3. extremely   4. outside   5. merrily   6. here   7. tommorow   8. downstairs   9. seldom   10. well

Grammar concept 5 : Prepositions 介詞

A preposition is a word used in front of a noun to show where, when or how something happens.

介詞用在名詞前面，以表示處所、時間、狀態、方式等。

漫畫看一看

When can you bring back the novel I lent you last week? I need to return it to the library in three days.

Will you be here on Saturday? I can bring it back to you.

No, I'll be at home at the weekend. You can come over at any time on Saturday.

I'll see you on Saturday morning at 9 o'clock then.

Alright.

❓ 文法解讀與辨析

時間介詞放在動詞後面，說明事情或動作發生的時間。

時間介詞	用法
at	帶出確切的時間或節日
on	帶出日期和特定日子
in	帶出一段頗長的時間

✅ 實用例句齊來學

at

- The film starts **at** 10:30 a.m. 電影在早上十時三十分開始放映。
- We arrived at the beach **at** sunset.
  我們在夕陽之際來到海灘。
- They usually stay with us **at** Christmas.
  聖誕節他們通常和我們在一起。

on

- Dad doesn't need to work **on** Sundays.
  爸爸周日不需要工作。
- I bought a new school bag **on** my birthday.
  生日那天我買了一個新書包。

in

- Benny was born **in** June. 賓尼六月出生。
- It's very cold **in** winter. 冬天很冷。
- I started learning the guitar **in** 2022. 我 2022 年開始學結他。

⚠️ 增潤知識大放送

在一天的不同時段，at 用於 at noon（在中午）、at night（在夜裏）、at midnight（在深夜），而 in 則用於 in the morning（在早上）、 in the afternoon（在下午）、in the evening（在晚上）。

漫畫看一看

❓ 文法解讀與辨析

位置介詞用來帶出事情發生的地點，最常用的也是 at、on 和 in，三者都解作「在」。

位置介詞	用法
at	帶出一點的位置
on	帶出平面和比一點大的空間
in	帶出圍住或相對更大的空間

✅ 實用例句齊來學

at

- I'll meet you **at** the bus stop. 我會在巴士站跟你碰面。
- The cat lay down **at** my feet. 這隻貓躺在我的腳邊。

on

- The answers are **on** page 100. 答案在第一百頁。
- We sat down **on** the ground. 我們坐在地上。
- Your dinner is **on** the table. 你的晚餐已經上桌了。

in

- What's **in** the box? 盒子裏有什麼？
- They used to live **in** Thailand, but now they're somewhere **in** Japan. 他們以前在泰國居住，但現在住在日本某個地方。

⚠ 增潤知識大放送

on 和 in 都可用來表示「乘車」，巴士或大型交通工具用 on，汽車或的士則用 in。例如：

- We're **on** the bus / train / plane. 我們在巴士 / 火車 / 飛機上。
- Who is **in** the car / taxi? 汽車 / 的士裏的人是誰？

漫畫看一看

Grammar 規則你要知

❓ 文法解讀與辨析

以下介詞也可用來表示事物的位置。

位置介詞	意思
in front of / behind	在前面 / 後面
on the right / left of	在右面 / 左面
above / under	在上面 / 下面

✔ 實用例句齊來學

in front of / behind

- Don't put your bicycle in front of the door.
  不要把單車放在門前。

- The boy hid himself behind the sofa.
  男孩躲到沙發後面去了。

on the right / left of

- The kindergarten is on the right of the post office.
  幼稚園在郵政局的右邊。

- Who is sitting on the left of Anna? 誰坐在安娜左邊？

above / under

- The plane is flying above the clouds. 飛機在雲層上飛行。

- Please put your bag under your chair. 請把袋放在椅子下。

⚠ 增潤知識大放送

right 和 left 本身可作形容詞用，例如：my left eye（我的左眼）、his right arm（他的右臂）。

在美式英語中，behind 可以說成 in back of，例如 Bill is sitting behind Terence.（比爾坐在泰倫斯後面。）可以說成 Bill is sitting in back of Terence.

漫畫看一看

Look! There is a butterfly.

Oh, it's flown out of the window!

It's flying towards the tree. Let's go down to catch it.

It's flying away from the tree now.

I'll get you and put you into a bottle.

We should never hurt any living things.

Grammar 規則你要知

❓ 文法解讀與辨析

方向介詞用來表示事物移動的方向。

方向介詞	意思
away from / towards	離開某處 / 朝某方向移動
into / out of	進入 / 離開
up / down	由下而上 / 由上而下

✔ 實用例句齊來學

away from / towards

- The prince walked **away from** the castle. 王子離開了城堡。
- A bird is flying **towards** us. 一隻鳥向着我們飛過來。

into / out of

- Let's go **into** the garden for a walk. 我們去花園散步吧。
- An orange rolled **out of** the bag. 一個橙從袋子裏滾出來。

up / down

- The cat ran **up** the tree. 貓兒跑到樹上去。
- The old woman fell **down** some stairs and broke her wrist. 老婦在樓梯上滑了一跤，手腕骨折了。

⚠ 增潤知識大放送

towards 特別用於英式英語，美式英語通常用 toward，字尾沒有 s。

作為介詞，out of 可引申指「不在（某個地方）」或「不處於（某種情況）」。例如：

- Mrs Lee is **out of** town this week. 李太太這星期不在城裏。
- The patient is now **out of** danger. 病人現在脫離了危險期。

漫畫看一看

❓ 文法解讀與辨析

介詞 by 的意思是「被」，解釋某人的動作或誰做了這個動作，用於被動語態的動詞之後。除此之外，by 也可用來表示某人採用何種方式來做某事，或誰是作家、作曲家、畫家等。

介詞	意思	用法
by	被；由	表示由誰做某事，與被動語態連用
	通過；使用	表示所用的方式
	由……所作	表示誰是作家、作曲家、畫家等

✔️ 實用例句齊來學

表示由誰做某事

- The zebra was eaten **by** the lion. 斑馬被獅子吃掉。
- The car was driven **by** an old man. 那輛汽車由一個老人駕駛。

表示所用的方式

- You can reserve the tickets **by** phone. 你可以使用電話訂票。
- We travelled to Guangzhou **by** high-speed train.
  我們乘搭高鐵去廣州。

表示作家、作曲家、畫家等

- *The Ugly Duckling* was written **by** Hans Andersen.
  《醜小鴨》由安徒生所著。
- This piano concerto was composed **by** Mozart.
  這首鋼琴協奏曲由莫札特作曲。

⚠️ 增潤知識大放送

by 很多時候會用在被動語態中，後接施行者，這施行者通常是有生命的個體，如以上例句的 lion、an old man、Hans Andersen、Mozart。

漫畫看一看

Chris, what are your plans for this summer?

I'm going to Taiwan with my parents.

Taiwan?

Well, I'll visit my grandma there. Look!

So this old woman with silvery grey hair is your grandma?

Yes. I'll probably stay with her for two weeks.

❓ 文法解讀與辨析

介詞 with 有多重意思，用法如下：

介詞	意思	用法
with	被；由	表示覆蓋或裝有，與被動語態連用
	使用；以	表示工具或方法
	和；跟隨	表示和……在一起
	有	表示擁有

✅ 實用例句齊來學

表示覆蓋或裝有

- The room was littered with toys. 房間裏玩具扔得到處都是。
- The books are covered with dust. 這些書本滿是灰塵。

表示工具或方法

- Wipe the table with a cloth. 用布擦一下桌子。
- Join the two pieces together with glue.
  用膠水把這兩塊黏在一起。

表示和……在一起

- She lives with her grandparents. 她和祖父母一起生活。
- I always wear these boots with this dress.
  這雙靴子我總是和這條裙子一起穿搭。

表示擁有

- Who's that man with long hair? 那個長髮男人是誰？
- I like that jacket with a hood. 我喜歡那件有兜帽的夾克。

⚠ 增潤知識大放送

在被動語態句子中，雖然施行者往往由 by 帶出，但也會用上 with。with 的意思同樣是「被」，用於描述狀態，而不是施行者，如以上第一、二句例句。

There is a mistake in each of the following sentences.
Underline and correct them in the spaces provided.

下列句子均有一處錯誤，請在錯誤部分下方畫線，
並在橫線上寫上正確答案。

1 My sister's birthday is at 8th August.

2 Stay away of me!

3 An apple rolled out from the bag.

4 This book is translated from a famous author.

5 Seal the package up by sticky tape.

6 They travelled across China with train.

7 The door was opened and a stranger came onto the room.

8 There is a park in front to the museum.

9 Dad's office is at the right of the shopping mall.

10 He was standing in the top of the stairs.

參考答案：1. at → on 2. of → from 3. from → of 4. from → by 5. by → with
6. with → by 7. onto → into 8. to → of 9. at → on 10. in → at

Grammar concept 6 :
Conjunctions
連接詞

A conjunction is a word that joins words, phrases and clauses of a sentence.

連接詞把句子中的詞語、片語和子句連接起來。

連接詞：and / but / or
Conjunctions: and / but / or

❓ 文法解讀與辨析

連接詞 and、but 和 or 把句中不同意思的部分連接起來。

連接詞	意思	用法
A and B	A 和 B；A 然後 B	連接相同部分
A but B	A 但是 B	表示相反意思
A or B	A 或 B	表示兩項中選一項

✅ 實用例句齊來學

A and B

- Zoey **and** Joey are twins. 柔伊和祖兒是雙生兒。

- He took a shower **and** went to bed. 他先洗澡，然後睡覺。

A but B

- Junk food is yummy **but** not very healthy.
  垃圾食物很好吃，但不太健康。

A or B

- Which do you prefer, ice cream **or** cheesecake?
  你想要哪一個，冰淇淋還是芝士蛋糕？

- Do you like to go camping **or** watch a film?
  你想去露營還是看電影？

⚠️ 增潤知識大放送

在英語，用 and 連接我和某人時，I 要放在 and 後面，即是我們不說 I and Tom，而說 Tom and I，例如：

- Tom **and** I usually play basketball on Sundays.
  湯姆和我通常會在星期天一起打籃球。

漫畫看一看

Grammar 規則你要知

❓ 文法解讀與辨析

連接詞 because 和 so 用來表示因果關係，because 說出原因，so 說出結果。

連接詞	意思	用法
because	因為	說出原因
so	所以	說出結果

✅ 實用例句齊來學

because

- I didn't go out **because** it was raining.
  我沒有外出，因為外面下雨。

- I made myself a sandwich **because** I was feeling hungry.
  我給自己做了份三文治，因為我餓了。

so

- It was raining **so** I didn't go out.
  外面下雨了，所以我沒有外出。

- I was feeling hungry **so** I made myself a sandwich.
  我餓了，所以我給自己做了份三文治。

⚠️ 增潤知識大放送

在中文，「因為……所以……」通常在同一句句子中連用，但英文只能使用其一。例如我們不說 Because she was tired so she went home. 而說 She went home because she was tired.（她回家了，因為她累了。）或 She was tired so she went home.（她累了，所以她回家了。）

because 通常放在句子中間，但當它置於句首時，後面的子句開始前須加上逗號。例如：

- **Because** she was tired, she went home.

連接詞：although / though
Conjunctions: although / though

漫畫看一看

Can I copy down your answers?

Yes, you can, though I'm not sure if they're right.

They couldn't be wrong. You're the smartest student in our class.

Although I come first in class, it doesn't mean I won't make mistakes.

Come on, Robert! You should finish your homework by yourself.

Grammar 規則你要知

❓ 文法解讀與辨析

連接詞 although 或 though 用來表示「雖然；儘管；即使」，在句子中扮演轉折的角色，說出令人意外的事情。它們通常會放在句首，後面的子句開始前須加上逗號。當放在句中時，前面通常不會加逗號。

連接詞	中文	用法
although / though	雖然；儘管；即使	表示意外的結果

☑ 實用例句齊來學

放在句首

- Although I'm full, I still want to eat.
  雖然我很飽，但我還是想吃東西。

- Though the sun was shining, it wasn't that warm.
  雖然有陽光，但天氣不太暖和。

放在句中

- I still want to eat although I'm full.
  我還是想吃東西，雖然我很飽了。

- She travelled on her own though she knew it could be dangerous. 她獨自旅行，儘管她知道可能會有危險。

⚠ 增潤知識大放送

在中文，「雖然……但是……」很自然在同一句句子中出現，但英文只能使用其一。例如我們不說 Although he was ill, but he still went to school. 而說 Although he was ill, he still went to school. 或 He was ill, but he still went to school.（雖然他生病了，但是他仍然去上學。）

113

漫畫看一看

Shall we watch this horror film?

No, if I watch something scary, I'll get nightmares.

Hey, relax. My friend said it is a very good film.

Well, I can watch it unless there're no ghosts in it.

Grammar 規則你要知

❓ 文法解讀與辨析

連接詞 if 用來表示「如果」，unless 用來表示「除非」，兩者都用來帶出條件。

連接詞	意思	用法
if	如果	帶出條件
unless	除非	帶出條件

✅ 實用例句齊來學

if

- I will tell you the secret **if** you promise to keep it to yourself.
  如果你答應保守秘密，我就把秘密告訴你。

- You'll get fat **if** you don't stop eating.
  如果你繼續吃下去，你就會變胖。

unless

- I won't tell you the secret **unless** you promise to keep it to yourself. 除非你答應保守秘密，否則我不會把秘密告訴你。

- You'll get fat **unless** you stop eating.
  除非你停止進食，否則你會變胖。

⚠ 增潤知識大放送

unless 跟 if...not 意思一樣。例如：

- You won't catch the ferry **if** you **don't** hurry.
  你要是不趕快，就趕不上渡輪了。

- You won't catch the ferry **unless** you hurry.
  除非你趕快一些，否則會趕不上渡輪。

unless 後面一定為肯定句，否則會造成雙重否定句。例如以上句子不能說成 You won't catch the ferry unless you don't hurry.

漫畫看一看

Hi Emma, I'm going shopping today. Do you want to come?

I can go with you after I finish my homework.

Sure. No problem.

I feel hungry. Shall we eat something before we go?

That's a good idea.

❓ 文法解讀與辨析

連接詞 before 和 after 表示事情發生的先後順序，before 指「在……之前」，after 指「在……之後」。兩者都可以放在句子開頭或句子中間。若放在句子開頭，就要加逗號來分隔後面的主要子句。若置於句中引導子句，則不用加上逗號。

連接詞	意思	用法
before	在……之前	後接之前發生的事情
after	在……之後	後接之後發生的事情

☑ 實用例句齊來學

before

- **Before** Nancy went to bed, she brushed her teeth.
  南希刷了牙才睡覺。

- She hugged everyone **before** she left.
  她離開前給每個人擁抱了一下。

after

- **After** I left you, I went to the library.
  離開你之後，我去了圖書館。

- We will go to the park **after** we finish our dinner.
  我們吃完晚餐後，就會去公園。

⚠ 增潤知識大放送

before 或 after 前可直接加上副詞來加強語氣。例如：

- I went to the police station *immediately* **after** I lost my wallet.
  我丟了錢包後，立刻去了警察局。

- *Shortly* **before** we set off, Leo said he felt sick.
  在我們出發前不久，利奧說他感到身體不適。

漫畫看一看

Grammar 規則你要知

❓ 文法解讀與辨析

when 和 while 用來連接有時間關係的子句，when 指
「當……的時候」，while 指「與……同時」。

連接詞	意思	用法
when	當……的時候	搭配有延續性或瞬間、短暫的動作
while	與……同時	只搭配有延續性的動作或情境

✅ 實用例句齊來學

when

- **When** I was about to leave, the phone rang.
  我正要離開時，電話響起來了。

- They were shocked **when** I told them the news.
  當我把消息告訴他們時，他們非常震驚。

while

- **While** she is drawing, she often listens to music.
  她時常在畫畫時聽音樂。

- The students came to the room **while** the teacher was
  waiting. 學生進入課室時，老師正在等候着。

⚠️ 增潤知識大放送

when 和 while 有時可以混用。當一個背景動作正在進行中，
同時發生了另一件事，這時用 when 或 while 都可以。例如：

- **When / While** I was watching TV, my sister rang the bell.
  我看電視時，妹妹按了門鈴。

當兩個動作都會延續一段時間，而非瞬間完成，通常就會
用 while。例如：

- **While** I was watching TV, my sister was sweeping the
  floor. 我看電視時，妹妹在掃地。

漫畫看一看

The film is about to start. Should we wait until Emma's here?

Is she coming?

I called her half an hour ago and she said she was reading a novel.

Oh, no. Once she starts reading she won't stop till it's done.

Let's get in or we'll miss the beginning of the film.

❓ 文法解讀與辨析

連接詞 until 和 till 表示「一直做某件事直到某個時間」。

連接詞	中文	用法
until / till	直到……為止	後接事情終結的時候

✔ 實用例句齊來學

- You don't know what you can achieve **until** you try.
  你還沒有嘗試，哪會知道自己能取得什麼成就。

- He was the headmaster **until** he retired two years ago.
  他一直擔任校長，直至兩年前退休。

- We stayed in the library **till** the library closed.
  我們待在圖書館直至關門為止。

⚠ 增潤知識大放送

until 一般不放在句子開頭，而放在句子中間。例如我們不說 Until the show ended, no one left the theatre. 而說 No one left the theatre until the show ended.（演出結束前，沒有人離開劇院。）

用 until 連接的句子，主句一般會用將來式。例如：
- We will wait **until** the rain stops. 我們會等到雨停為止。

但要注意，即使 until 引導的子句說明將來的情況，子句還是會用現在式或完成式，而不用將來式。例如以上句子不能說成 We will wait until the rain will stop.

漫畫看一看

❓ 文法解讀與辨析

有些連接詞必須一對地使用，兩組詞語不能分開，請看看下表。

連接詞	用法
either **A** or **B**	不是 **A**，就是 **B**
neither **A** nor **B**	既不是 **A**，也不是 **A**
both **A** and **B**	**A** 和 **B** 都是
not only **A** but also **B**	不僅是 **A**，而且是 **B**

☑ 實用例句齊來學

- Lily wants to learn **either** Japanese **or** Korean.
  莉莉想學習日語或韓語。

- Mr Smith **neither** smokes **nor** drinks.
  史密夫先生既不抽煙，也不喝酒。

- **Both** John **and** Jason love reading.
  約翰和賈森都很喜歡閱讀。

- David is **not only** tall **but also** strong.
  大衞不僅個子高，而且很強壯。

⚠ 增潤知識大放送

若 either A or B 或 neither A nor B 所引導的主詞為名詞，動詞的單複數必須隨 or 或 nor 之後的名詞的單複數對應，例如：

- **Either** you **or** Tom **has** to sweep the floor.
  不是你就是湯姆得要掃地。

- **Either** you **or** the girls **have** to clean the house.
  不是你就是這些女孩得要打掃房子。

Fill in the blanks with the correct conjunction.

請在橫線上填寫正確的連接詞。

1 Chloe didn't come to school _____ she was sick.

2 Neither my mother _____ my father speaks English.

3 Joseph is very hardworking _____ not very imaginative.

4 _____ we make a decision, does anyone want to say anything else?

5 Adrian felt not _____ upset but also heartbroken.

6 Most wild animals won't attack _____ they are provoked.

7 They came to our home _____ we were having dinner.

8 My knee started hurting _____ I stopped running.

9 _____ she knew it was difficult, she decided to give it a try.

10 You will feel cold _____ you do not dress warmly enough.

綜合練習 1
Integrated exercise 1

Choose the correct answer for the following sentences.
Tick the correct box.

請為下列句子揀選正確的答案，並在 ☐ 內加 ✓。

1 This jacket is too small. I need a (☐ A. smaller ☐ B. larger ☐ C. more large) size.

2 The shoes were quite cheap. I expected them to be (☐ A. much more ☐ B. much ☐ C. less) expensive.

3 Frank is (☐ A. the bad ☐ B. worst ☐ C. the worst) student in our class.

4 Could you please shut the door (☐ A. quiet ☐ B. more quiet ☐ C. quietly)?

5 I'm not old enough to drive, but my (☐ A. more old ☐ B. older than ☐ C. elder) brother has got a car.

6 Yesterday was (☐ A. the cold ☐ B. the coldest ☐ C. coldest) day of the year.

7 Jessica wants to learn (☐ A. either ☐ B. neither ☐ C. both) the piano or the guitar.

8 The students waited in the classroom (☐ A. while ☐ B. until ☐ C. though) the rain stopped.

9 Water turns to steam (☐ A. unless ☐ B. until ☐ C. if) the temperature hits 100°C.

10 (☐ A. While ☐ B. When ☐ C. After) I was doing my homework, my brother was watching TV.

綜合練習 2
Integrated exercise 2

Fill in the blanks with the correct modal verb.

請在橫線上填寫正確的情態動詞。

1 Mum says we _____ watch TV after we've finished our homework.

2 His bike broke down in the middle of nowhere, but luckily he _____ to fix it.

3 You _____ leave your door unlocked when you go out.

4 You don't _____ pick me up at the airport. We can get a taxi.

5 I'm not sure what I will do for my holidays, but I _____ go to the beach.

6 Today is your birthday. _____ we go out for dinner tonight?

7 You _____ be tired because you have worked very hard.

8 He _____ love singing, but he doesn't do it any more.

9 How _____ she shout to her mother?

10 _____ you like some coffee or tea?

參考答案：1. can 2. was able 3. shouldn't / ought not to 4. need to 5. may / might 6. Shall 7. must 8. used to 9. dare 10. Would

綜合練習 3
Integrated exercise 3

There is a mistake in each of the following sentences.
Underline and correct them in the spaces provided.

下列句子均有一處錯誤，請在錯誤部分下方畫線，
並在橫線上寫上正確答案。

1 I enjoy to talk to my grandparents. _____

2 It were very kind of him to offer me his coat. _____

3 Smoke is harmful to your health. You must stop it. _____

4 My father sometimes lets me going to his office. _____

5 Please don't make me to stay at this horrible place. _____

6 Would you mind speak more slowly, please? _____

7 Are you frighten of spiders? _____

8 It will be a very excited experience for you. _____

9 There are lots of butterfly among the flowers. _____

10 Bill is still ill but he looks a lot more good than the day before. _____

參考答案：1. to talk → talking　2. were → was　3. Smoke → Smoking
4. going → go　5. to stay → stay　6. speak → speaking
7. frighten → frightened　8. excited → exciting
9. butterfly → butterflies　10. more good → better

綜合練習 4
Integrated exercise 4

There is one word missing in each of the following sentences. Put a caret (∧) to indicate its place in the sentence and write the word in the spaces provided.

下列句子均有一個字詞不見了，請在相應位置加入插入符號 (∧)，並在橫線上寫上該字詞。

1. They agreed visit the museum on Saturday.
   _____

2. Longest river in Africa is the Nile.
   _____

3. You need have a passport to visit most foreign countries.
   _____

4. The film starts 4 o'clock.
   _____

5. Don't stand in front the TV.
   _____

6. The supermarket is on right of the school.
   _____

7. We are sitting far away each other.
   _____

8. *Hamlet* written by Shakespeare between 1599 and 1602.
   _____

9. I was feeling thirsty I bought a can of Coke to drink.
   _____

10. Janet is not only beautiful also intelligent.
    _____

參考答案：1. visit → to visit 2. Longest → The longest 3. have → to have 4. 4 o'clock → at 4 o'clock 5. in front → in front of 6. on right → on the right 7. away → away from 8. written → was written 9. I bought → so I bought 10. also → but also

Irregular verbs
不規則動詞

- 包括小學階段常用的 150 個不規則動詞。

- 括弧內的動詞與 he、she、it 或其他單數名詞同用。

- 限於篇幅,每個動詞只附帶一個中譯。

Present simple 現在式	Present participle 現在分詞	Past simple 過去式	Past participle 過去分詞
ache (aches) 疼痛	aching	ached	ached
advise (advises) 勸告	advising	advised	advised
agree (agrees) 同意	agreeing	agreed	agreed
apologise (apologises) 道歉	apologise	apologised	apologised
argue (argues) 爭論	arguing	argued	argued
arrange (arranges) 排列	arranging	arranged	arranged
arrive (arrives) 到達	arriving	arrived	arrived
bake (bakes) 焗	baking	baked	baked
be (am / is / are) 是	being	was; were	been
beat (beats) 打敗	beating	beat	beaten / beat
become (becomes) 變成	becoming	became	become
begin (begins) 開始	beginning	began	begun
behave (behaves) 表現	behaving	behaved	behaved
believe (believes) 相信	believing	believed	believed
bend (bends) 弄彎	bending	bent	bent
bite (bites) 咬	biting	bit	bitten
blame (blames) 責備	blaming	blamed	blamed
bleed (bleeds) 流血	bleeding	bled	bled
blow (blows) 吹	blowing	blew	blown
break (breaks) 打碎	breaking	broke	broken
breathe (breathes) 呼吸	breathing	breathed	breathed
bring (brings) 帶來	bringing	brought	brought
build (builds) 建築	building	built	built
burn (burns) 燃燒	burning	burned / burnt	burned / burnt
buy (buys) 購買	buying	bought	bought

Present simple 現在式	Present participle 現在分詞	Past simple 過去式	Past participle 過去分詞
catch (catches) 捕捉	catching	caught	caught
chat (chats) 閒談	chatting	chatted	chatted
choose (chooses) 選擇	choosing	chose	chosen
clap (claps) 拍手	clapping	clapped	clapped
close (closes) 關閉	closing	closed	closed
come (comes) 來	coming	came	come
cry (cries) 哭	crying	cried	cried
cut (cuts) 切	cutting	cut	cut
cycle (cycles) 騎車	cycling	cycled	cycled
damage (damages) 破壞	damaging	damaged	damaged
decide (decides) 決定	deciding	decided	decided
decorate (decorates) 裝飾	decorating	decorated	decorated
dig (digs) 挖	digging	dug	dug
do (does) 做	doing	did	done
donate (donates) 捐贈	donating	donated	donated
draw (draws) 繪畫	drawing	drew	drawn
dream (dreams) 做夢	dreaming	dreamed / dreamt	dreamed / dreamt
drink (drinks) 喝	drinking	drank	drunk
drive (drives) 駕駛	driving	drove	driven
eat (eats) 吃	eating	ate	eaten
exercise (exercises) 做運動	exercising	exercised	exercised
fall (falls) 落下	falling	fell	fallen
feed (feeds) 餵飼	feeding	fed	fed
feel (feels) 感覺	feeling	felt	felt
fight (fights) 打架	fighting	fought	fought

Present simple 現在式	Present participle 現在分詞	Past simple 過去式	Past participle 過去分詞
find (finds) 找到	finding	found	found
fly (flies) 飛	flying	flew	flown
forget (forgets) 忘記	forgetting	forgot	forgotten
forgive (forgives) 原諒	forgiving	forgave	forgiven
freeze (freezes) 結冰	freezing	froze	frozen
get (gets) 取得	getting	got	gotten / got
give (gives) 給	giving	gave	given
go (goes) 去	going	went	gone
grow (grows) 成長	growing	grew	grown
guess (guesses) 猜想	guessing	guessed	guessed
hang (hangs) 掛	hanging	hung / hanged	hung / hanged
hate (hates) 憎恨	hating	hated	hated
have (has) 有	having	had	had
hear (hears) 聽見	hearing	heard	heard
hide (hides) 躲藏	hiding	hid	hidden
hit (hits) 打	hitting	hit	hit
hold (holds) 拿住	holding	held	held
hope (hopes) 希望	hoping	hoped	hoped
hug (hugs) 擁抱	hugging	hugged	hugged
hurt (hurts) 弄傷	hurting	hurt	hurt
imagine (imagines) 幻想	imagining	imagined	imagined
invite (invites) 邀請	inviting	invited	invited
jog (jogs) 慢跑	jogging	jogged	jogged
keep (keeps) 保留	keeping	kept	kept
kiss (kisses) 吻	kissing	kissed	kissed

Present simple 現在式	Present participle 現在分詞	Past simple 過去式	Past participle 過去分詞
kneel (kneels) 跪下	kneeling	knelt / kneeled	knelt / kneeled
knit (knits) 編織	knitting	knitted / knit	knitted / knit
know (knows) 知道	knowing	knew	known
lay (lays) 下蛋	laying	laid	laid
lead (leads) 帶領	leading	led	led
learn (learns) 學習	learning	learned / learnt	learned / learnt
leave (leaves) 離開	leaving	left	left
lend (lends) 借出	lending	lent	lent
let (lets) 讓	letting	let	let
lie (lies) 說謊	lying	lied	lied
lie (down) (lies) 躺下	lying (down)	lay (down)	lain (down)
light (lights) 點火	lighting	lit / lighted	lit / lighted
like (likes) 喜歡	liking	liked	liked
lose (loses) 遺失	losing	lost	lost
love (loves) 愛	loving	loved	loved
make (makes) 做	making	made	made
meet (meets) 會面	meeting	met	met
pay (pays) 付款	paying	paid	paid
plan (plans) 計劃	planning	planned	planned
prepare (prepares) 準備	preparing	prepared	prepared
put (puts) 放	putting	put	put
quarrel (quarrels) 爭吵	quarrelling	quarrelled	quarrelled
read (reads) 閱讀	reading	read	read
reply (replies) 回答	replying	replied	replied
ride (rides) 騎	riding	rode	ridden

Present simple 現在式	Present participle 現在分詞	Past simple 過去式	Past participle 過去分詞
ring (rings) 發出鈴聲	ringing	rang	rung
rise (rises) 上升	rising	rose	risen
rub (rubs) 擦	rubbing	rubbed	rubbed
run (runs) 跑	running	ran	run
saw (saws) 鋸	sawing	sawed	sawn / sawed
say (says) 説	saying	said	said
see (sees) 看見	seeing	saw	seen
sell (sells) 賣	selling	sold	sold
send (sends) 寄出	sending	sent	sent
sew (sews) 縫製	sewing	sewed	sewn / sewed
shake (shakes) 搖動	shaking	shook	shaken
shine (shines) 發光	shining	shone	shone
shoot (shoots) 射擊	shooting	shot	shot
shop (shops) 購物	shopping	shopped	shopped
show (shows) 展示	showing	showed	shown
shut (shuts) 關閉	shutting	shut	shut
sing (sings) 唱歌	singing	sang	sung
sink (sinks) 下沉	sinking	sank	sunk
sit (sits) 坐	sitting	sat	sat
sleep (sleeps) 睡覺	sleeping	slept	slept
slide (slides) 滑行	sliding	slid	slid
smell (smells) 聞到	smelling	smelt / smelled	smelt / smelled
smile (smiles) 微笑	smiling	smiled	smiled
spit (spits) 吐痰	spitting	spat	spat
speak (speaks) 説話	speaking	spoke	spoken

Present simple 現在式	Present participle 現在分詞	Past simple 過去式	Past participle 過去分詞
spend (spends) 花費	spending	spent	spent
spell (spells) 拼寫	spelling	spelt / spelled	spelt / spelled
spill (spills) 溢出	spilling	spilt / spilled	spilt / spilled
stand (stands) 站立	standing	stood	stood
steal (steals) 偷	stealing	stole	stolen
sweep (sweeps) 打掃	sweeping	swept	swept
swim (swims) 游泳	swimming	swam	swum
swing (swings) 搖擺	swinging	swung	swung
take (takes) 拿着	taking	took	taken
teach (teaches) 教	teaching	taught	taught
tease (teases) 取笑	teasing	teased	teased
tell (tells) 告訴	telling	told	told
think (thinks) 認為	thinking	thought	thought
throw (throws) 拋	throwing	threw	thrown
tidy (tidies) 整理	tidying	tidied	tidied
try (tries) 嘗試	trying	tried	tried
travel (travels) 旅行	travelling	travelled	travelled
understand (understands) 明白	understanding	understood	understood
use (uses) 用	using	used	used
wake (wakes) 醒來	waking	woke	woken
wear (wears) 穿	wearing	wore	worn
win (wins) 贏	winning	won	won
wish (wishes) 希望	wishing	wished	wished
worry (worries) 擔心	worrying	worried	worried
write (writes) 書寫	writing	wrote	written

趣味漫畫學英語

小學漫畫 Grammar 王：Grammar 文法篇 1

作　　　者：Aman Chiu
繪　　　圖：黃裳
責任編輯：黃稔茵
美術設計：劉麗萍、徐嘉裕
出　　　版：新雅文化事業有限公司
　　　　　　香港英皇道 499 號北角工業大廈 18 樓
　　　　　　電話：(852) 2138 7998
　　　　　　傳真：(852) 2597 4003
　　　　　　網址：http://www.sunya.com.hk
　　　　　　電郵：marketing@sunya.com.hk
發　　　行：香港聯合書刊物流有限公司
　　　　　　香港荃灣德士古道 220-248 號荃灣工業中心 16 樓
　　　　　　電話：(852) 2150 2100
　　　　　　傳真：(852) 2407 3062
　　　　　　電郵：info@suplogistics.com.hk
印　　　刷：中華商務彩色印刷有限公司
　　　　　　香港新界大埔汀麗路 36 號
版　　　次：二〇二四年七月初版

ISBN: 978-962-08-8406-1
© 2024 Sun Ya Publications (HK) Ltd.
18/F, North Point Industrial Building, 499 King's Road, Hong Kong
Published in Hong Kong SAR, China
Printed in China